Laura E. H. Richards

Jim of Hellas

In durance vile. Bethesda pool

Laura E. H. Richards

Jim of Hellas
In durance vile. Bethesda pool

ISBN/EAN: 9783337387143

Printed in Europe, USA, Canada, Australia, Japan

Cover: Foto ©Andreas Hilbeck / pixelio.de

More available books at **www.hansebooks.com**

JIM OF HELLAS

OR

IN DURANCE VILE

––––

BETHESDA POOL

BY

LAURA E. RICHARDS

AUTHOR OF "CAPTAIN JANUARY," "MELODY," "QUEEN HILDEGARDE,"
"FIVE-MINUTE STORIES," "WHEN I WAS YOUR AGE,"
"NARCISSA," "MARIE," "NAUTILUS."

𝔗𝔢𝔫𝔱𝔥 𝔗𝔥𝔬𝔲𝔰𝔞𝔫𝔡

BOSTON
ESTES AND LAURIAT
1895

Typography and Printing by
C. H. Simonds & Co.
Electrotyping by Geo. C. Scott & Sons
Boston, U. S. A.

TO MY

Dear Brother,

HENRY MARION HOWE,

THIS VOLUME

IS AFFECTIONATELY

DEDICATED.

JIM OF HELLAS

JIM OF HELLAS.

Part I.

EVERYONE knows the Island; it is not necessary to name it. With its rolling downs, its
points, its ponds, its light-houses, and above all, its
town,—who does not know the Island? Some day
1 shall write a story about the downs, the billowy
acres of gold on russet, russet on gold, wonderful
to see,— but this story is about the town.

The town has its nominal government, like other
towns; its selectmen, and its town-meeting, and
other like machinery; but everybody knows that the
real seat of government lies in the Upper House.
The meetings of this republican House of Lords are
held in the best room of "Bannister's," the one inn
of the town. It is a pleasant, roomy old structure,
built in the Island fashion, with wide windows and
plenty of them, and with a railed platform on its flat-
topped roof, from which, in former days, the women

of the house used to watch for the coming of the whaling-fleet.

There is little watching now on the Island. No ships come into that wonderful harbour, once thronged with sails. The great wharves rot silently and fall apart; a few old hulks rot quietly beside them. Two or three fishing-smacks, a coal-schooner or two,— these are all one sees now from the roof or the windows of Bannister's.

But the men who sit together in the upper room still look out of the windows a great deal, because from them they can see the harbour, and beyond it the sea; and the sea is what they love best to look at, for the greater part of their lives has been spent on it. Old sea-captains,— it needs but one glance to tell of what the Upper House is composed: Men with faces that might have been carved out of mahogany, wrinkled and seamed and beaten into strange lines by wind and weather; with gray or white hair, for the most part, and shaggy beards, yet with keen, bright eyes which are used to looking, and, what is not always the same thing, to seeing what they look at.

Though most of them go to sea no more, they keep with care their sea-going aspect; they wear pea-jackets with huge horn buttons, heavy sea-boots, and never fail to don their sou'westers in bad weather.

The room in which they sit is well suited to them. On the broad window-seats lie spy-glasses and telescopes of all kinds. The walls are hung with sea-trophies.

Here is a piece of plank transfixed by the sharp blade of a sword-fish; there, a pair of walrus-tusks; there, again, the beautiful horn of the narwhal, like a wonderful lance of ivory, fit weapon for King Olaf or Eric the Red. In the doorway stands a whale's jaw, a great arch ten feet high, under which all must pass with thoughts of Jonah. As for corals and shells, there is no end to them, for the upper room is a museum as well as a place of convention, and here the captains love to bring their choicest treasures, keeping only the second-best to adorn the chimney-piece of the home-parlour.

In a great arm-chair, facing a seaward window, sits the patriarch of the Upper House, old Abram Bannister. His grandfather had built the inn itself, his grandsons now keep it. Every morning, winter and summer, Jake and Bill "hist" the old captain out of bed, put him in his chair, and wheel him into the great room; then they give him a spy-glass to hold in his hand, and leave him till dinner-time. The captains begin to straggle in about eight o'clock, when their morning chores are done. They greet the white old man with never-failing cordiality; he is the pride of the Upper House. They are never tired of asking him how old he is, nor of hearing him reply in his feeble, cheery pipe, —

"Ninety-nine year, and risin' a hundred."

He sleeps a good deal of the day, and, on waking, never fails to cry out, "Thar' she blows!"

Whereupon, one of the captains promptly replies, "Where away?" and the patriarch says, —

"Weather bow!" and straightway forgets all about it, and plays with his spy-glass.

When the captains are assembled in sufficient number, they discuss the affairs of the town, talk over this or that question, and decide what the "se-leckmen" ought to do about it.

Woe to the selectmen who should dare to oppose the decision of the Upper House! Something dreadful would happen to them; but, as they never have opposed it, one cannot tell what form the punishment would take.

Now it fell, on a day, that the captains were sitting together spinning yarns, as was their custom when business was over. The present and the immediate future provided for, it was their delight to plunge into the past, and bring up the marvellous treasures hidden in that great sea. Captain Zeno Pye was telling about the loss of the "Sabra" in the year 1807. His father had been on the vessel, and Cap-

tain Zeno sometimes forgot that it was not himself,
so often had he told the story. The other captains,
sitting like so many veiled prophets, each shrouded
in his cloud of smoke, listened with the placid enjoy-
ment of connoisseurs, making a mental note of any
slightest variation of word or inflection in the
familiar narrative. Any one of them could have told
it in his sleep, but it was Captain Zeno's story, and
·it was one of the unwritten laws of the Upper House
that no captain should tell another's story.

"So," said Captain Zeno,—he was a little walnut-
faced man, with sharp black eyes, and a dry and
rasping utterance,—"so they was makin' good sailin'
with a fair wind, on the 18th day of October, when
all of a suddent the lookout sung out—"

"Thar she blows!" broke in Captain Abram, in
his piping treble.

"Where away?" responded Captain Silas Riggs,
promptly.

"Weather bow!" said the old man, and fell silent
again. All looked at Captain Zeno, who smiled
appreciatively.

"Won'erful, aint it?" he said, meditatively. "He
knows that pint, Cap'n Abram does, as well as I do.
Wal, as I was sayin', they struck a school o' whales,
on the weather bow, sure enough; sperms they was,
and likely-lookin' fur as they could see. Three

boats put off, and my father, bein' mate at that
time, had one of 'em. He sighted a sixty-barrel
bull, and was pullin' for him for dear life, when
an old cow come by with her calf, and when she
saw the boat she dove, and one eend o' the fluke
struck 'em amidships, and stove a hole in 'em.
Wal! that kerwumpussed 'em, ye see! Nothin'
for it but to pull back to the ship, and set to work
on repairs. My father called the carpenters, and
give 'em their job, an' then he looked after the
school, and cussed a little, mebbe, for all he was
a perfessor, to think he was losin' all the fun.
All of a suddent he seed a whale leave the school,
turn round, and make straight for the ship. He
didn't think nothin' of it, 'cept he see 'twas the
biggest bull his eyes had ever come across. Big?
Wal!' 'Twas like a island, Father used to say. He'd
heerd tell of two-hundred-and-thirty-barrel whales
along back in the seventeens, and he calc'lated this
might be one of 'em left over. He see the critter
was comin' pooty nigh, and he sung out for a
harpoon, thinkin' he might git a shy, after all;
when, lo ye! that whale took a start an' come
through the water like a shot out of a gun, and
struck the ship just forrard of the forechains.

"Wal, sir, they was knocked consid'able eendways,
I tell ye! Father was dumfoundered for a minute,

and the ship's crew with him, what with the surprise
on't, and the everlastin' shakin' it giv 'em, too. But
Father never let his wits go without a string tied to
'em, and in a minute he ordered all hands to the
pumps, to see if she had sprung a-leak. She hed, sir;
she was sinkin'; and Father run up the sign for the
boats to come back. He turned round from runnin'
up that signal, and you may call me a Jerseyman if
the whale wasn't comin' for 'em agin, head on and
all sails drawin'! Before Father could sing out, he
struck 'em again, pooty nigh the same place, with a
crash that sent every man-jack sprawlin' on his face.
Wal, sir, 'twas boats then, 1 can tell ye, and no time
to lose, neither! Th' other boats kem back and took
'em aboard, and in five minutes' time the 'Sabry'
down with her nose and up with her heels, and down
she went to Davy. Yes, sir! That's what you
might call — "

At this moment the captain was interrupted by a
knock at the door. He looked displeased, but said
" Come aboard!" with as good a grace as he could;
while the other captains turned cheerfully in the
direction of the knocker, who might bring them
something new in place of a many-times-told tale.

A lank, ungainly man entered, and stood timidly
on one foot, with his mouth open, holding the door
in his hand.

"Come aboard!" repeated Captain Zeno, impatiently. "Shet the door! Say yer say with yer mouth, and then shet that, — if ye can get it all to at one't!" he added, in an undertone.

The ungainly man looked slowly round the room, and stroked his lantern-jaws. "That man!" he said, deliberately, lingering on each word as if it were too precious to part with, "what be I to do with him?"

The captains looked at one another. They had been speaking of this matter only a few minutes before, but they feigned unconsciousness.

"What man do you mean, Sefami Bunt?" asked Captain Zeno, severely. "The prisoner who was caught stealin' hens from Palmyry Henshaw last week?"

The man nodded. "Says he wants somethin' to do!" he said. "Says he'd like to do chores round for his victuals. Says he does n't like my victuals."

The captains chuckled. Sefami Bunt was a bachelor, and his housekeeping was not supposed to be of a high order.

"Have ye got him in the jail?" asked Captain Asy Bean.

The lantern-jawed man shifted uneasily to the other foot. "Wal, I hev!" he admitted. "But he does n't seem to be contented with that." Then, after a pause, "I brung him with me. 'T want safe to

leave him, for the jail door sags so I can't lock it,
and the chain is bust. So 'f you 'd like to see him
for yerselves —"

" Where is he?" asked the captains in chorus.

Sefami Bunt gave a backward jerk with his head.
" I tied him to the leg o' the table," he said. " The
boys is mindin' of him. Sh'll I fetch him up?"

Receiving an affirmative answer, he disappeared,
and returned, dragging the prisoner by the collar.

The latter, the instant he caught sight of the
assembly of mariners, shook off his keeper with a
single movement; then, making his obeisance in true
seaman fashion, he glanced quickly round the room,
and stood still, cap in hand, in an attitude of respect-
ful humility.

He was a short, thick-set man, evidently of great
strength; a sailor, every inch of him, from the gold
rings in his ears to the way he set his feet down.
Jet-black curls clustered about his brown, smiling
face. His dark eyes were alive with intelligence and
humour. His open shirt displayed a neck elaborately
tattooed, while hands and wrists were a museum of
anchors, hearts and crosses.

" Will you speak to him, Cap'n Bean?" said one
or two of the other captains in low tones.

" Wal, I don't want to be settin' myself up,"
replied Captain Asy, " but if it 's the wish" — he

glanced round the circle, and ascertained that it was the wish. Whereupon, clearing his throat and assuming a quarter-deck frown, he asked, in majestic tones, " What is your name, prisoner ? "

The dark eyes looked intelligence. " Name, honourable captains ? Giorgios Aristides Evangelides Paparipopoulos."

" Great Andes ! " exclaimed Captain Asy. " We 've got the whole archipelago, and no mistake. What do they *call* ye ? Hey ? "

" Ah ! "— the brown face flashed into a bewildering smile, an ivory revelation. " Call me ? Jim ! "

The captains breathed again.

" That 's more civilized ! " said Captain Asy. " Now, you Jim, what have you got to say for yourself ? "

It appeared that Jim had a great deal to say for himself. He was not happy, he must inform the honourable captains. He complained of his quarters, of his jailer, of his fare. He had, it was true, stolen a hen, being very hungry and having no money to seek the so honourable hotel. The hen was almost uneatable, but — he had stolen her. He had been condemned to three months' imprisonment in the jail, and it was well. But — here he waxed eloquent, pathetic. " I haf been in jail, honourable captains, before. Never for great offence, but — I have been.

But never like zis! Ze rain come in upon my bed.
I try to shut ze door, for ze wind blow at me, but he
not shut. I sleep, and ze ship come in ze door and
eat me."

"Hold on there!" said Captain Asy. "What do
you mean by that? Hey? Ship come in the
door?"

"Yes, honourable captain; t'ree gre't big ship. I
hear 'baa! baa!' I wake suddainlee, and zey are eat
my foot."

"Sheep, he means!" the jailer explained. "The'
warnt but two, I guess. Fact, they got a way o'
wand'rin' int' the jail, but they would n't ha' hurt him
any. He's dretful skeered for one that's knocked
about pooty nigh the world over, from what he says."

"But!" the prisoner maintained, turning a candid
face upon the court: "is it a jail — for ship to walk
in and eat — what you say neeble — ze foots of
prisoners?"

"No! no! 'taint!" "That's so!" "He's right,
gentlemen!" came from the assembled captains.

"Zen," Jim continued, "ze mess! Salted backbone
of hog — must I eat always zis? Never for t'ree
mont's ozer sing? Honourable captains, I die."

"Wal!" said Sefami Bunt, with a hint of bluster
in his voice, "I guess if backbone 's good enough for
me, it's good enough for him! 'T was a good hawg!
and, anyway, I 've got to use it!"

"Sold the rest and salted down the backbone for yourself and prisoner?" queried Captain Asy Bean.

The jailer nodded, and repeated in an injured tone:

" 'T was a good hawg! Anybody could ha' seen him fattenin' any time they mind to pass by."

"And I tell Mr. Bont,"—Jim resumed the thread of his narrative, smiling apology around,—"I tell him, 'Let-a me go!' not ron avay, of course; 1 cannot ron avay if I wish. It is island. I tell him 'Let-a me go and work! I make ze door good; I mend ze windows; I do for ozer people work, perhaps zey give me ozer mess.' Is it not?" with a sudden flash and gleam of eyes and teeth.

There was a short pause. "How did you come here, anyway?" queried Captain Bije Tarbox.

It appeared that Jim had fallen overboard from his vessel. It was night, and his fall had not been noticed. Fortunately, the vessel was, even at the moment, passing the Island. He was a good swimmer, used to being in the water for a long time—briefly, behold him! He stole the hen. He was taken, brought before the "selected gentlemen." That was his story.

"Just step outside with Bunt a minute, my man," said Captain Asy Bean, "and we'll settle your case." Then, as the door closed behind the smiling criminal and his gloomy guardian, Captain Asy turned to the others:

"Gentlemen, this story may or may not be true. It sounds fishy; but, anyhow, the man must have come from somewhere, and I d'no as it matters much, s' long as he 's here now. Question is, what to do with him now he *is* here. Just like them *seleck-men*, lettin' the jail go to rack an' ruin, an' then clappin' a man in thar for the sheep to nibble."

"Man 's a seaman, anyhow," said Captain Bije Tarbox. "Ought t' ha' been sent straight to us."

"That 's so!" assented the captains all.

"Wal!" resumed Captain Asy, "'pears to me the straight thing is for us to send for the *seleckmen* — they 'll be goin' by to dinner direckly, an' we can toll 'em in an' say to 'em —"

"Thar she blows!" sang out Captain Abram.

"Where away?" asked Captain Moses Packard.

"Weather bow!" was the reply; and then the talk went on again.

Part II.

MISS PALMYRA HENSHAW was sitting in her neat kitchen, with folded hands. The kettle was singing cheerfully, the cat was purring contentedly by the stove; but for once Miss Palmyra's mood did not chime in with the singing or the purring. She had sprained her ankle the day before, and it was now so painful, that, after dragging it about till her work was "done up" (for, land sakes! she couldn't sit down in the dirt; and her kitchen had to be cleaned up, if she did it on her hands and knees), she was fain now to sit down and put the offending member up on a chair.

She looked at the poor foot with great displeasure. It was badly swollen; she had had to put on a green carpet slipper, one of an old pair of her father's; and the contrast with her other foot, in its trim, well-blacked shoe, was anything but pleasant.

As she sat thus in silent discomfort, she heard the sound of the pump in the yard. Somebody was working the handle up and down with firm, regular strokes.

"Well, what next?" said Miss Palmyra, fretfully,

peering out of the window and trying to gain a sight of the intruder. "I sh'd like to know who's at that pump without askin' leave or license. I left the pail out there, too, did n't I? Like as not it 'll go, same as the hen did. I must get up!"—she made a motion to rise, but sank back with a groan. "My Land! Have I got to sit here and have my things stole without liftin' a finger?"

At the same moment she heard quick steps crossing the yard: the door opened, and a man entered, carrying a brimming pail of water. Miss Palmyra opened her mouth to shriek, but closed it again when the stranger smiled.

"Good eve!" said the man, who had black curls, gold rings in his ears, and the brightest eyes that ever were seen. "I come to do ze work."

"Work!" ejaculated Miss Palmyra, faintly.

"Ze shores!" explained the man, with a brilliant flash of eyes and teeth. "You have hurt ze foot? So peety! Look! I fill ze kettel—so! I bring ze wood—so!" (He was gone, and back again with an armful of wood before Miss Palmyra could trust her bewildered senses enough to know whether she was awake or dreaming.) "I fill up ze stofe—so! And next? It is a cow zat you haf? I milk her!" He swept a glance around the kitchen, seized with unerring instinct the right pail, and was gone again.

Miss Palmyra pinched herself, and opened and shut her eyes several times.

"I wonder if I'm goin' crazy!" she said. "I feel kinder light-headed."

She looked at the cat, who blinked quietly in return, and his calm air of tranquillity steadied her nerves. "If he'd been a tramp, he wouldn't ha' brought in that wood!" she said. "Would he, Eben?" The cat was named Ebenezer. Ebenezer purred assurance, and Miss Palmyra's spirits rose. "Like as not he's stayin' with some o' the neighbours!" she said. "Mis' Brewster's real kind: mebbe this is her nephew she was expectin', and she sent him in to help me. Well, I'm sure!" She twitched a little shawl over the carpet-slipper, and settled her neat collar and apron.

When the stranger returned, beaming over the brimming milk-pail, she was able to greet him with "Well, you're real obligin', I must say. I didn't hardly know what I should do about milkin', for I can't seem to put my foot to the ground. Stayin' at Mis' Brewster's, be ye?"

"No!" with a flash which illuminated the kitchen. "Not zere. Where he live, ze milk? Zis door?"

Miss Palmyra indicated the pantry door, where the yellow pans stood ready and waiting.

She listened keenly for a sound of spilling or drip-

ping, but none came; only a steady, even pouring.
"He's a real good hand!" she murmured.

"And now?" the dark eyes smiled on her again.
"You lame, I get your sopper. What you like?"

"Oh,—no, sir, you can't do that!" cried Miss
Palmyra. "I'm jist as obliged, I assure *you*, but I
sha'n't want nothin' more to-night. I had a good
dinner. Well, I'm sure!"

She felt utterly helpless when the stranger, with
another smile, produced three eggs from his pocket,
and taking a bowl, proceeded to break the eggs into it
and beat them with right good will. "When you
seeck, then you weak," he explained. "Most eat
good sopper! I make!"

In the twinkling of an eye the frying-pan was
on the stove; and, while it was heating, his keen
black eyes spied a tray. Napkin, knife and fork
were arranged upon it with swift precision. Setting
a plate to warm on the back of the stove, he
proceeded to do wonderful things with the beaten
eggs, tossing them about with a fork, stirring,
seasoning, tasting. This was done with the right
hand, while the left was toasting a slice of bread.
All the time the black eyes were glancing here
and there, like darting sunbeams. Spying a string
of onions, the stranger pounced upon them. A
morsel was torn off, shredded fine, and stirred into
the savoury mess.

In five minutes such an omelette was smoking on the hot plate as Miss Palmyra had never even dreamed of; and in one minute more it was beside her on the little light-stand, and she was bidden "Eat! I make tea!"

Now Miss Palmyra had *not* had a good dinner, and she was desperately hungry, and — oh! how good that omelette did smell! The toast was perfect!

Where had Mis' Brewster's nephew learned all this? And now, to crown all, a cup of tea was set beside her, — hot, strong and fragrant. And then —

"Please ze lady I also have a cup?" asked this astonishing person. The tone was soft and pleading, the dark eyes deprecating, as if he were a humble suitor, asking a royal boon.

"Well, I should hope you could!" cried Miss Palmyra, hospitably. The idea! I don't see what I was thinking of, Mr.— *Is* your name Brewster?"

"No!" said the stranger, softly. "Name is Jim!"

A good supper had Giorgios Aristides Evangelides Paparipopoulos, *alias* Jim, that night! There was more omelette than Miss Palmyra could possibly eat, she declared; indeed, Jim had meant that there should be. Then she told him where to find a certain loaf of spice cake, and a jar of damson jam; and she insisted upon his eating till he could eat no more. After a week of salted backbone of hog, Jim's appetite for these good things was keen enough.

He beamed with pleasure; his smiles made noon-day in the darkening kitchen: Miss Palmyra thought him uncommonly handsome. Only — it was a pity he wore ear-rings. And, after all, who was he? She really must find out.

"You 've never told me how you kem to know of my bein' lame!" she said, as her guest was washing the dishes with careful nicety. "You a stranger here, too! Who did send ye, if I 'm not takin' a liberty?"

"Ze honourable captains send me," said Jim, with open cheerfulness; "and ze selected gentlemen."

"Well, I 'm sure!" ejaculated Miss Palmyra.

"I steal your hen!" Jim explained, with winning grace. "Was very sorry; should not have done — but! Now I work t'ree mont'; do shores for ladies; do all works. But for you I work most, for I steal your hen. Is it not?" And putting away the cups and saucers, he swept the hearth with ardour.

"Well, I 'm sure!" said Miss Palmyra again; and she really could not think of anything else to say.

Everyone agreed that it was a special providence that Jim Popples (such being the popular rendering of our hero's name) had been cast away on the Island just when there was so much sickness "goin' about," and when Aunt Ruhamy Snell, the accredited nurse of the Island, was laid up with rheumatism. The quick, active Greek was here, there and everywhere. He split wood, he made fires, he milked cows. He mended chairs, and set panes of glass; he kept all the children happy by plaiting wonderful things out of twine, and whittling royal navies with his jackknife.

He also mended up the jail as well as he could, and might be seen patching the walls of his cell, whistling merrily, while the jailer sat by in moody silence watching him. It was generally felt that Sefami Bunt had not done as he ought by his prisoner, and that he really was not fitted for the offices he held of jailer and hog-reeve; but, as Captain Zeno Pye said, "thar warnt nothin' else Sefami *could* do, and it kep' him off the town, anyway."

But Jim's best work, and his longest hours, were given to Miss Palmyra Henshaw. She had freely forgiven him his theft of the hen, and in the long period of inactivity to which she was now condemned (for if one trifles with a sprained ankle, one is apt to pay for it, and it was a month before she could do more than hobble about with a crutch), she found him an invaluable friend. Morning, noon and night would see him smiling at the door, with his cheery "How you do, Mees Palmyre? So better, is it not? Glad I am!"

Often he brought some little offering: a wooden dish of wild strawberries; a string of fish, gleaming fresh from the water; or it might be half-a-dozen crabs, which would crawl out of his pockets, only to meet a swift death in the kettle of boiling water, and be converted into some wonderful dish. Of Jim's skill in cookery, Miss Palmyra spoke with bated breath.

"Well!" she would say to Mrs. Brewster, who, toiling over her own cook stove, sometimes wished she had a sprained ankle and could have Jim Popples to do her work; "that man has a real gift, that 's sartin'. Give him an egg and an onion, and it does seem as if he could git the flesh-pots of Egypt out of 'em. Jest you step to the cupboard, Mis' Brewster. Thar's a corner I left special for you to taste, a dish o' tomaytoes and rice he cooked for my dinner yesterday. Just them, and a bit o' butter and a scrap of onion, and—thar! Did you ever! Don't that relish good?"

Small wonder that Miss Palmyra grew plump and rosy in spite of the sprained ankle.

Many a housewife wished, like Mrs. Brewster, that she also might profit by Jim's gift; but though he did all kinds of chores for the whole village, he would cook for no one but Miss Palmyra Henshaw. "I steal you hen!" he said to her. "I wish to make you up for zat. I steal hens at no ozer lady."

So Miss Palmyra grew to feel a sort of ownership

of Jim Popples, which was by no means unpleas-
ant; and she sewed on his buttons (for pleasure;
he could do it perfectly well himself, as she
knew) and mended his clothes; while he, at work
with broom or mop, or whittling away at basket-
splints, told her wonderful stories of foreign lands, of
apes and peacocks, cedars and pomegranates, till the
good woman grew to feel that her thief was a very
remarkable and very gifted person.

So three months slipped away, as fast as months
are apt to do; and a day came when the captains sat
all together in the Upper House at Bannister's, and
Giorgios Aristides Evangelides Paparipopoulos stood
before them, as he had stood once before, with his
jailer glooming beside him.

The captains had sent for him, and now, at a
murmur from the others, Captain Zeno Pye took up
the word:

"Wal, Jim, yer three months is up, and I s'pose
you're thinkin' about goin'. Me and the captains
feel to say to you that you've done well, real well. Of
course you started in mean, and stealin' aint right,
however you look at it. But you've worked stiddy,
and you've worked good; and I reckon you'd have to
hunt round consid'able before you found anybody in
town who wa'n't real sorry to have ye go. If you
felt to stay, I don't doubt but you could get all the

work you wanted, odd-jobbin' round. The seleck-
men 'd oughter pay ye somethin' for repairin' the jail,
but thar! — that's between you and them. Wal!
the steamer comes to-morrer, and I s'pose you'll be
movin'. What we want to say is, that we're right
sorry to have ye go, Jim Popples. You're a handy
fellow, and I don't doubt you're a good seaman;
and if me or the other captains can speak a good
word for ye, or help ye any way with a start, why,
we're ready to do it. That's so, aint it?"

There was a growl of assent, in the midst of
which —

"Thar she blows!" sung out Captain Abram
Bannister.

"Where away?" cried Captain Bije Tarbox.

"Weather bow!" responded Captain Abram, and
slept peacefully.

Jim looked slowly round the circle; his smile grew
wider and brighter, till each man felt warm, and
thought the weather was moderating; then he saluted
in seaman fashion.

"I not go!" said the child of Hellas. "I stay.
I get married to-morrow — to Mees Palmyre!"

THE TROUBLING OF BETHESDA POOL

THE TROUBLING OF BETHESDA POOL.

SOME people in the village (but they were the spiteful ones) used to say that Bethesda Pool might e'en so well be a dummy and done with it, if she never could open her mouth when a person spoke to her. But there were always others who were ready to respond that "it was a comfort there was one woman who knew enough to hold her tongue when she had nothing to say!" This retort was apt to provoke the reply churlish; and many a pretty quarrel had been hatched up over the silence of Bethesda Pool, who never quarrelled herself, because it entailed talking.

She was the Lady of the Inn, Miss Bethesda. Her mother, the late Mrs. Pool, had married the innkeeper, and led a sad life of it. She was a woman of a lively fancy, and had been in the habit of saying that if she had been fool enough to get drownded in a pool, she meant to get all the good she could out of the name! So she named her eldest daughter Siloama (pronounced Silo-amy), her second Bethesda, and the son, who came just after her husband had drowned himself in his special pool of whiskey, Heshbon.. The neighbours thought this triflin' with Scriptur', and had their own opinion of Ma'am Pool's eccentricities; but the good lady cared little for any-body's opinion; indeed, if she had had any such care, she would not have married Father Pool, whose failings were well known. All that was long ago, however; Father and Mother Pool were gone to their places, the pensive Silo-amy and the fishy Heshbon had followed, and Miss Bethesda was Queen of the Inn.

The Inn was the only one in the village. Perhaps there was little need even of this; but it had always been there since the old stage-coach days, when the village was a favourite stopping-place for gay parties of travellers, and when old Gran'ther Pool kept open house, and smiled over his bar on all comers, like a rising sun a little the worse for wear. It was a quaint old house, with a stone veranda in front, and mossy roofs pitching this way and that. Inside was maze upon maze of long, narrow corridors, with queer little rooms opening out of them, — some square, some long; all low of ceiling and wavy of floor, with curious dolphin-shaped latches, and doors set as if the builder had thrown them at the wall and made the opening wherever they happened to strike. Few of these doors were on a level with the floor; they might be two steps above it, or three steps below; it was a matter of fancy, purely. There was one room that could only be entered through the closet, unless you preferred to get in at the window; but you could easily do that, as it opened on the balcony. Then there was a square chamber containing a trap-door; the Kidderminster carpet fitted the trap perfectly, and it was a dangerous room for strangers to enter. Here the Freemasons used, in old times, to hold their meetings, and carry on their mystic rites. Later, it was the favourite playroom of the Pool children, and they and their playmates were never tired of popping up and down the "Tumplety Hole," as they called it.

In the middle of the second story was a long ball-room, where in old days merry dances had been held, and young feet jigged it to the tune of " Money Musk " or " Hull's Victory."

This room, with its wonderful wall-paper, repre-senting the Carnival at Rome, and its curious clock, was an object of wonder to the whole village; and strangers or visitors were pretty sure to present them-selves at the Inn door, sometimes begging to be taken in for a few days, sometimes merely asking the privilege of going over the quaint old house. The reception of these visitors was apparently a matter of caprice with the Lady of the Inn; one never could tell how she would take it. Sometimes an eager statement that "We heard of your beautiful house, and we have driven over from South Tupham, ten miles, on purpose to see it!" would be met by the monosyllable "Have!" delivered in Miss Bethesda's mildest tone, and the door would be softly but firmly shut in the travellers' faces. Or the visitor might try another tack, and begin with the bold assumption that the Inn was a place of public entertainment, and that man and beast were welcome there, as a matter of course.

"I should like two bedrooms and a sitting-room, please! And will you send someone to look out for my horses? And—I should like supper, something hot, as soon as convenient!" To which Miss Bethesda might reply, "Should you?" and smile, and again shut the door.

But there were other times when something in the asking face or voice touched one knew not what chord in the good lady's breast. On these occasions she could be very gracious, and would say, perhaps, that she really did n't know, she did n't take boarders— mebbe— just this once— if' t would accommodate— she didn't know— but she might compass it somehow, and the door would be opened wide; and, once

inside, the guest was sure to be made so comfortable
that he was loth to go away again.

The fact was, that being clothed with means, as
they say in the village, the Lady of the Inn felt that it
was merely a matter of personal fancy, the taking in
of guests, and that if she were not in the mood for
visitors there was no manner of reason why she
should be bothered with them.

She had one servant, a grim elder, by name Ira
Goodwin. The spiteful people before alluded to said
that Ira — or Iry, to give the name its actual pronun-
ciation — and his mistress never spoke to each other,
but communicated by means of signs. That could not
be true, however, for Mrs. Peake, next door, had been
shaking a carpet in her yard one day, close by the
fence, and had heard Iry say, in a growling manner,
" Guess I can hold my tongue as well as others!"
To which Miss Bethesda's crisp tones replied:
" You'd better, for the outside of your head does you
more credit than the inside!"

Thus Miss Bethesda Pool lived in solitude for the
most part, and content with her lot; and no breeze
ruffled the still waters of her life.

It was very peaceful to be alone there in the great
rambling Inn, and hear no sound save the purring of
the yellow cat, and the drip of the water from the
roofs. The roofs all leaked in the Inn, whenever

there was a possible chance for leaking, and the walls were covered with strange patterns and hieroglyphics that were not included in the design of the wall-paper.

It happened one day that Miss Bethesda Pool was sitting in her own comfortable room, toeing off a stocking, and thinking of many things, when she heard a knock at the door. She took no notice of the first summons, for she found that in many cases the knocker, after one, or at most two, trials, was apt to go away, which saved a world of trouble, and showed that he had no business that amounted to any-thing, anyhow. But this was a persistent knocker, who kept on with a timid yet steady " rat-tat-tat—" till Miss Bethesda concluded that, whoever it was, he had not sense enough to know when he was n't wanted, and that she must answer the knock.

She folded her knitting deliberately, and after ex-amining the draughts of the stove, and stroking the yellow cat two or three times, she went to the door, holding her chin a little high, and looking, if the truth must be told, rather uncompromising.

When she opened the door, however, the lines of her face softened and her chin went down. A bright-faced girl stood there, with a shawl wrapped round her, for the day was cold. She was trying to smile, but there were tears in her brown eyes, and her lip was quivering.

"Miss Pool," she said, "I don't suppose I can come in, can I? I'd like ever so much to speak to you, if you would n't mind!"

Miss Bethesda opened the door wide, and without wasting breath, led the shivering child in, and closed the door after her with a bang. That bang carried defiance across the way, and gave Miss Bethesda as much comfort as if she had let loose a torrent of angry words. There is great comfort in a door sometimes. Still in silence, she led the girl into the sitting-room, drew a chair near the stove for her, and motioned her to sit down. Then resuming her own seat, she took up her knitting again, and gazing calmly on her visitor, evidently felt that she had done her part.

"It's Father, Miss Pool!" said the pretty girl, whose name was Nan Bradford. Miss Pool nodded comprehension, and set her lips more firmly. "Father, he's going on dreadful!" said Nan. "You know Will Newell has been—well, he has thought a sight of me, and I of him, these two years past.

"It came about while I was staying to grandma's, over to Cyrus, and grandma knew all his folks, and there aint any better folks in the country, grandma said. And yet—Father—he acts as though Will was one thief and I was another. He won't

let him come to the house, nor he won't let
me write to him, nor he won't do anything—
'cept just be ugly! There! I had n't ought to
say it, I know,—my own father, and just as good
a father as ever a girl has in the wide world, I do
believe, till this come up. But he won't hear of
my marrying anybody,—that is the plain truth,
Miss Pool, not if it was a seraph with six wings!
And—and—what am I to do, I should like to
know? I come to you, 'cause you 've always been
good to me, and I seem to know you better than
anyone else, now grandma's dead. And I would n't
complain of Father to anyone else in the village,
so I would n't!"

She paused for breath; Miss Pool looked at
her and nodded. It was an expressive nod, and
the girl seemed to feel better for it. She began
to cry softly, wiping her pretty eyes with the
corner of her shawl. "I'm just beat out!" she
said, plaintively. "Be!" said Miss Bethesda, sooth-
ingly; and she went to the cupboard and brought
out some of the famous cookies which a few
privileged children were allowed to taste from
time to time, but seldom anyone who had passed
the boundary of childhood. Nan, who was still a
child in some ways, brightened at sight of the
cookies, and was soon nibbling them in comparative

comfort, sighing from time to time, and glancing
up under her long eyelashes at Miss Bethesda,
who sat knitting as if her life depended upon it,
her lips set very tight, and apparently taking no
notice of her guest. But Nan Bradford knew Miss
Pool, and was content to wait. She would not
have been let in, she knew, if the Lady of the Inn
had not been in a good mood. So she nibbled the
cookies, and thought of Will, and was as comfortable
as a lovelorn and persecuted damsel could be.

Miss Bethesda kept her eyes fixed on her work,
but she did not see it. Instead of the gray wool
and shining needles, a stalwart figure stood before
her, the figure of Buckstone Bradford. He had
been her neighbour for all the years of their life;
he was four years her senior, and they had been
playmates in childhood. A breezy, rosy-cheeked
boy he had been, and her sworn ally. The children were apt to divide into two parties: Bethesda
and Buckstone on one side, Siloama and Heshbon
on the other. Thus arrayed, they were wont to do
battle around the yawning gulf of the Tumplety
Hole, shouting their respective war-cries, which
alluded, in an unfriendly spirit, to the qualities of
the enemy.

> "Gruff and Grum!
> Deaf and Dumb!"

Siloama and Heshbon would pipe shrilly; to which Bethesda and Buckstone would reply, in deeper tones,

> "Snively, Sneaky,
> Wobbly, Weaky!"

A general combat would ensue, in the course of which both parties were apt to fall down the trap-door into the basement room below, and be rescued by Mother Pool, and summarily dealt with by her slipper.

Then came the days of youth, when Buckstone courted her, and might have won her if he had gone to work in the right way. But he was headstrong, and she was obstinate; and he didn't get on with Siloama, and he was hard on Heshbon, and so it had all blown over; he had married another wife, and lost her while Nan was a baby. Miss Bethesda had forgotten all about Nan by this time: before her stood the man of her choice, with his feet apart and his chin stuck out, much as her own sometimes was; his brows were knit, his eyes gleamed with sombre fire.

"Bethesda," he said, and the words seemed to force the way through his strong white teeth, "Bethesda, I'm going to marry you, anyway, and I'd like to see you get out of it! Mind that!"

Ah, well, that was all men knew! She had got out

of it, — was it a sigh that came at the thought, or a
sniff of triumph, or a combination of the two? And
Buckstone had married a pindlin' soul that had n't no
more life in her than a November chicken — and —
that was all there was to it, Miss Bethesda reckoned.

And now, here he was hectoring this little girl of
his, that always favoured him, and had no look of her
mother — hectoring and bullying, just as he used;
and Miss Bethesda wondered if the child was a-going
to stand it. She would n't have stood, it not a day,
for her part, if she was his daughter, let alone his —
his — wife! And then she found herself wondering
whether he would have been so hectoring if she had
been — and brought herself up again with an indig-
nant start. Why in Tunkett should she be fretting
herself about Buck Bradford's girl, she wanted to
know! And yet, — she had got the better of Buckstone Bradford once; it would beat the world if she
could put him down again, would n't it?

While these thoughts were passing through her
mind, the Lady of the Inn sat, to all appearance,
absorbed in her work, never dropping a stitch, never
failing to count with the regularity of a self-respect-
ing clock; and Nan Bradford watched her anxiously
over the edge of her cooky.

"Miss Pool asks the pleasure of your company at a social dance, on Thursday evening, at seven o'clock.

"Yours truly,
"Bethesda Pool."

THIS was the bomb-shell that fell into every respectable household in the village two days after Nan Bradford's visit. Such a sensation had never been known since old man Pool rode a saw-horse across the common and into meeting the Sunday before he died; and, indeed, that was nothing to be compared to this. Bethesdy Pool! Bethesdy Pool *give a party!!* Well, what next? everybody wanted to know. Half-an-hour after the notes had been delivered by Iry Goodwin (who carried them round in a basket and handed them out as if they were death warrants), every woman in the village, with two exceptions, was in another house than her own.

"Have you got one?" "Have you?" "Let me see!" "Lemme see if 'tis like mine?" "Yes, they're all the same!" "Well, I do declare! don't you?" "Is the mile-ennion coming, or what, do you s'pose?" "A social dance! Bethesdy Pool, as hasn't set down to a table, nor yet asked a soul to set down to hers these fifteen years,—well of all! but so 't is! You can't tell where to have some folks, even though you've had 'em all your life, as you may say!"

The general verdict was that the Pools were all "streaky," and Bethesda the most streakèd of any of them; and that most likely she was going clean out of her mind this time, and there would be an end of it.

However, the unanimity on this point was equalled by the determination of everybody, old and young, rich and poor, to go to the party. In fact, it seemed probable that every house in the village would be deserted on the eventful evening; for not a soul was willing to lose the sight of a party in the old Inn.

Report said, as the day came nearer and nearer, that great preparations were going on. Every woman who had any skill in cookery had offered her services eagerly, hoping to have some share in the great doings; Mrs. Fullby had "presumed likely" that Bethesda would have more'n she could manage with her own two hands, and had assured her that she, Mrs. Fullby, would jis lives's not bring her apurn and eggbeater and put right in on the cake and frostin'! while Miss Virginia Sharpe hinted delicately that there was "a certain twist" in the making of pastry that

was considered peculiar to the Sharpe family, and that
no festivity would be complete without "Sharpe
tarts;" but Miss Bethesda was of the opinion that
she and Iry could do what was necessary, and just as
much obleeged to *them!* and in point of fact, not a
soul, with the exception of Nan Bradford, who was
seen to emerge once from the Inn, looking rather
frightened but very happy, was permitted to set foot
within the mysterious doors.   Mrs. Peake said that
she saw Nan coming home, looking as if she had seen
a ghost and lost her heart to it; but Mrs. Peake had
a poetic way with her, and her remarks were not
much heeded in the village.

It was thought more likely that Nan had been
poking her nose in where her betters would n't ha'
thought of poking theirs, and got it taken off for
her pains, and served her right! But it happened
that Mrs. Peake was right this time.

Thursday evening came!   The moon was full, the
sleighing perfect; Nature was evidently in league
with Miss Bethesda Pool, and meant to do her share
in making the party a success. Miss Pool, standing
in state at the end of the ballroom, waiting for her
guests to arrive, made a pleasant picture in her old-
fashioned flowered brocade, one of the self-supporting
kind, little beholden to any figure inside it. Her hair
was still brown, still pretty, with its crinkles that

caught the light, and gave her a wonderful look of youth, well carried out by her bright hazel eyes, and trim figure. In truth, she was not old, Miss Bethesda; her fortieth birthday was only just past, and she was straight as a dart, and strong as a tree; but when one has played old woman for fifteen years, one gets to think the play a reality, and one's neighbours are not slow to adopt the view. On looking in the glass, this evening, Miss Bethesda experienced a slight shock, and a decided impression of good looks. She wondered if Buckstone Bradford would find her much changed; she regretted that she had worn her old " punkin " hood quite so uniformly for the last ten years, and meditated on the attractions of a certain sky-blue " fascinator," which had been lying in her top-drawer ever since Siloama died. Fond of bright colours Siloama always was, and dressy to the day of her death. Anyhow, the brocade was handsome enough to please any one! Miss Bethesda smoothed down the shining folds, examined her white silk mitts carefully, and glanced up at the clock, to see how much longer she had to wait. Nearly seven! Folks would most likely be on time, Miss Bethesda thought, with a grim smile; curiosity could hurry the laziest folks that ever forgot to draw their breath! She reckoned every old podogger in the village would turn out to see Bethesdy Pool make a fool of herself; but let

'em come! There'd be more than one fool to-night,
if things went as they should! 'T was strange,
though, that she had n't heard no word from —

Here her meditations were interrupted; for the
door at the end of the ballroom flew open and re-
vealed a tall young man, wrapped to his eyes in fur,
who rushed forward and took her hand, and tried to
say something, and failed egregiously.

"Will Newell!" cried Miss Bethesda, "do you
mean to tell me this is you? For gracious sake, what
do you want? Did n't you get my note?"

"Yes, ma'am, I did," cried the big fellow, drawing
the sleeve of his fur coat across his eyes. "I've done
as you said; but I could n't go farther without thank-
ing you, not if 't was ever so! Miss Bethesda, I —
I'd do anything in the world for you, I believe. You
don't know what a time we've had,— Nan and me.
We — I — well, I'm not one to talk, never was! but
I *would* do anything for you, now, I would!"

"Dance the Virginia Reel with me, then," said
Miss Bethesda, smiling grimly at her joke. "Or else,
if you don't want to do that, take yourself out of this
as quick as you can, Will Newell, and get ready!
Hark! There's the bell this minute. You've fixed
it all right with Nan?"

"All right!" panted Will. "I've got the team hid
away where you said, in the old cow-shed. Now I'll

go and fix me; and maybe we will have the reel,
Miss Pool, if you'll have it early enough on the pro-
gramme. I won't promise to wait for you, though,
more'n the first half of the evening."

He ran out, his eyes shining with joy; and Miss
Bethesda folded her white mitts again, and waited
calmly for the first guests.

The clock struck seven, and Miss Bethesda glanced
up again. It was a wonderful clock, this of the old
Inn. More than a hundred years it had hung there,
having been brought over from England by Gran'ther
Pool, before he lost his money and took to keeping
the Inn. Its dial and frame were gayly painted with
dancing figures, with garlands of flowers, from which
peeped laughing faces of loves and fairies. The great
weights that hung against the wall were curious, too,—
dolphin-shaped, like the door-latches, and shining with
remnants of gilding. And now, following closely on
the seventh stroke, came notes of music, faint, rus-
tling notes, the very spirit of sound; a waltz, sweet
and delicate as the tiny faces that peeped from the
painted garlands on its dial, faltered forth from the
old clock : "Tra-la-la, lira-la, la-la!—" and between
the notes of the swinging measure the wheels creaked
and groaned, and the wires wheezed, and the weights
lamented as they slid up and down. "Just like any
other old fool," thought Miss Bethesda, "doing things

she has no business to!" and for a moment she felt
as old as the clock, and repented her of her purpose.

But the guests were here! They had been
gathering for some time in the cloak-room, and
now one couple had been bold enough to make
the first break, and the narrow staircase was crowded
with maids and matrons, sons and fathers, all in
their best. Every eye glistened with eager curiosity,
every mouth was open to whisper in the next ear
at anything singular that should meet the eye
when they came into their hostess's presence; but
lo and behold! there stood Bethesda Pool, looking
as if she had a party every week of her life, and
had nothing in the world to do but stand there
and look fine.

Very stately was the courtesy with which Miss
Bethesda greeted her guests. She was pleased to
see them; hoped they would enjoy themselves, and
make themselves as much to home as if they *was* to
home! This was generally the extent of her con-
versation with any one group of eager neighbours,
before turning to welcome the next. But presently
the colour deepened a little in her still fresh cheek,
and her eyes grew brighter; for, coming up the
ballroom, she saw the stalwart form of Buckstone
Bradford, with pretty Nan beside him, looking like
roses and milk in her white dress. "Knew he'd

come!" Miss Bethesda said to herself; and immediately discovered, by the flutter at her heart, that she had not known, but only hoped it.

Truth to tell, Mr. Bradford had had a dozen minds about coming to Bethesda Pool's party. He had never forgiven her for her treatment of him twenty years before; his heart was of firm and tenacious fibre, and retained the impression of affections and of injuries more than many a softer organ. He considered Bethesda still the finest-looking woman in the neighbourhood, and would have snorted with contempt if anyone had told him that his daughter Nan, with her pink-and-white prettiness, was fairer than ever his old sweetheart had been. But admiring was not forgiving, and nothing would have brought Buckstone out to-night save the dread of "goings-on" on the part of his girl and that good-for-nothing Newell fellow.

There was something in the air,—Buckstone did not know what it was,—something that made him uneasy. Nan had been so meek the last time he scolded her, never once standing up for her favourite, as she was wont to do; she had been so affectionate, and,—well, she was always a good girl when she wasn't making a fool of herself about a noodle; but there was more than usual, her father thought. He didn't dare to let her go alone to the party;

there was the plain truth of it; he was afraid, he knew not of what. So he had had his hair cut, and had taken out and brushed his wedding coat, not without angry and defiant thoughts of her who should have stood up with him when he wore it; and, briefly, here he was, standing before Bethesda Pool, grim and forbidding, but still a fine-looking man, his hostess thought, and towering head and shoulders above everyone else in the room.

"Good evening, Mr. Bradford! pleased to see you!"

"Your servant, Miss Pool!" and it was over, and the mist began to clear from Miss Bethesda's eyes, as she turned aside to ask the fiddler if he was ready. The fiddler was ready, of course. He had been tuning his fiddle for the last fifteen minutes, and his fingers were itching to begin. Was he not a pupil of old Jacques de Arthenay, the famous fiddler of the last generation? And had he not been shelved for the past ten years, just because folks were fools enough to prefer an organ and a cornet to the only instrument ordained of Heaven to make people dance! So with right good-will he mounted the stool in the corner, and struck up the "Lady of the Lake."

How many years it was since that hall had rung to the sound of a fiddle! Probably no one present

knew; but many, and especially the older ones, or
those who were cast in a sentimental mould, felt that
there was something ghostly in this first dance.
People were a little timid, perhaps; and their hostess,
standing silent and stately in her stiff brocade, was
not the one to set them at their ease. It seemed
to Miss Selina Leaf as if, when the dancers took
their places in the two long lines, she heard the
rustle of many gowns that were not seen in the
room; as if old, forgotten perfumes were wafted
through the air, and soft, subdued voices whispered
courtly greetings at her side. She was "littery,"
Miss Selina, and had written many "sweet things"
for the county weekly.

But the "Lady of the Lake" is a robust and
inspiring dance, and soon banished all shadowy or
sentimental thoughts from the minds of the dancers.
"Down the middle!" "Sashy to partners!" "Turn
the same!" "Eight hands round!"

Soon eyes were sparkling and cheeks glowing like
flame, and the young feet went flying up and down
the long, low room, as young feet will fly when the
fiddle sounds and the blood courses freely through the
veins.

Miss Bethesda Pool looked on with bright eyes, her
foot (she had the prettiest foot in the room, and knew
it) tapping in time to the music. She had refused

several invitations to dance, without a word, simply a sniff of denial; but it was good to see a dance again.

Will Newell was there, dancing with his cousin, the pasty-faced girl, who would have money when her grandfather died: dancing dutifully, as if the cousin were the only girl in the room, and not so much as glancing toward where Nan Bradford, more rosy than ever, was footing it lightly as a fairy, opposite young Jacob Flynt.

Jacob was her father's choice for her, as everybody knew; and it was no wonder that Buckstone Bradford looked cheerful and contented as he leaned against the wall with folded arms, watching the dancers.

Yes, Buckstone was contented for the moment; things were going just as he wished to see them; and yet — so ungrateful a creature is man — he could not help suspecting even his own satisfaction. What made Nan so happy? When had anyone seen her look like this before when she had to dance with Jacob Flynt? Was this duty or — or what?

The "Lady of the Lake" was followed by the "Portland Fancy;" that by the splendid romp of the "Tempest."

Ah! these were dances! Happy the neighbourhood where the real dances, the wreathing, linked garlands of grace and lightness and youth, still form part of a ball! The waltz is pretty enough, when well done;

but who has not tired of the endless whirl of revolving couples, dual teetotums, spinning round and round, till sight and brain are dizzy alike? You shall not find, in painting or sculpture, any showing forth of waltz or polka as Nature's expression of joy and motion. But what Greek vase or tablet, what glowing canvas of Giorgione, or Veronese, but might be glad to catch the rhythmic swing of the "Tempest," as the long line wavers to and fro, and the bold dancers in the middle sweep down the hall and back again,— to catch and fix it in immortal lines of carving or of colour?

"Gents choose partners for 'Pop goes the Weasel!'"

There had been an intermission, during which the hall had hummed like a hive of vari-coloured bees. People were thoroughly at ease now, and speech flowed freely, as the couples promenaded up and down.

"A festive occasion, truly, Mr. Bumpus!" said Miss Selina Leaf, with gentle dignity.

"Bustin'! bustin'!" replied Mr. Bumpus, with effusion. "Haven't seen such goin's on in the village, *I* d'no when! Does a person good to limber out the j'ints once in a while; dancin's better than bar's grease any day in the week! Haw! haw!"

Miss Selina considered this remark vulgar, and bridled gently, but made no reply.

"Surprisin' thing, too," Mr. Bumpus went on. "Bethesdy Pool — now, you 'd ha' said her dancin' days were over, if anyone had ha' asked you, would n't you, — same as yours and mine?"

Miss Selina winced again, and looked toward a seat, but the bold Bumpus went on, unconscious.

"We 'd ha' said that, surely, — you and me; yet there she is, looking most as young as the girls, I do maintain. Don't know as there 's any manner of use in gettin' old before you 're obleeged ter; never enj'yed a 'Lady of the Lake' more than I did that one with you, ma'am. What 's that? 'Pop goes the Weasel?' Now you don't mean to say! Why, I haint danced 'Pop goes the Weasel!' since my Maria was a baby, and look at her dancin' it with her husband! Reckon I must look up my woman and dance this with her, or she 'll be castin' up at you, Miss Selina; so if you 'll excuse *me!* —" and the good man bustled off, leaving Miss Selina rigid with indignation.

"Pop goes the Weasel!" It was an old dance, and had not been seen in the village for years. Indeed, many of the lads and lasses had never seen it, and looked about them at a loss, as the lively strains struck up, notes whose shrill gayety made even the "Tempest" seem quiet by comparison. But the older men

and women cast glances at each other, half-shy, half-
pleased. This was renewing old times with a ven-
geance! Many a husband followed the example of
Israel Bumpus, and led out the choice of his youth,
flattering himself that she "stood it as well as any of
'em," while mature spinsters settled themselves elaborately in their seats, with an air of never having
heard of the old-fashioned dance,—unless some one
came to ask them for it, in which case memory
became suddenly refreshed, and they stood up with
right good-will.

Now it happened that in happier days this had
been the favourite dance of Miss Bethesda Pool, and
that her favourite partner in it had been Buckstone
Bradford. She could not keep back a start when the
well-known air was played with all its old fire; and
for the life of her, it seemed, she could not help looking across the hall at Buckstone, where he stood, leaning stiffly against the wall. He was looking at her,
of course: somehow, she knew he would be. Their
eyes met; and perhaps neither of them knew exactly
what happened next. Before Mr. Bradford had time
to collect his thoughts, he found himself bowing his
stiff back before Bethesda Pool. "My dance, I
believe!" he said, shortly; and though Miss Bethesda
knew it was nothing of the kind, she could not find
breath to say so. She looked up, she looked down;

and the next moment, to the amazement of everybody, the two old sweethearts took their places at the head of the line.

Now Will Newell had been growing uneasy during the last half-hour. He had hardly had a chance to speak to Nan, yet had managed to make her understand that all was ready, and that when he gave the word she was to take her life in her hand and fly with him. But when could he give the word? Bradford's eyes had hardly left his daughter's figure all the evening; he followed her up and down the lines of dancers, frowning heavily if Will happened to be near her in the dance, stolidly content if her neighbour were young Jacob Flynt. What was Will to do? The horse would be getting uneasy, and the moon would be setting before long. He must get rid of old Bradford, somehow!

Suddenly, hardly able to believe his eyes, he saw his tormentor fairly turn his back on Nan: saw him cross the room, saw him bend before Miss Bethesda, saw him standing up to dance. Now! now was the chance! In an instant Will had forced his way before Jacob Flynt, who was just about to lead Nan out for the dance. "You're engaged to me for this, you know, Nan," said this unblushing young fellow; and he drew her arm under his with a quick, masterful gesture. "But—but—but she promised me!" cried poor Jacob, who stammered a little.

"Oh, go to Tinkham!" said Will, alluding dis-
respectfully to the next township; and he led off his
trembling Nan in triumph.

> "All around the cobbler's shop
> The monkey chased the weasel;
> That's the way the money goes, —
> *Pop!* goes the weasel!"

The fiddle-says "Pop!" as plainly as the ridiculous
doggerel; and at the word, two of the three who have
been swinging round together lift their arms, and the
third goes "*pop!*" under and rises to confront the next
couple: more tiptoe swaying, balancing to this one,
chassez-ing to that one; then three hands round, and
"*pop!*" goes the weasel again; and so on down the
whole room, in the prettiest, merriest, most enchant-
ing dance of them all. But this is engrossing, I
would have you know. When one is popping every
third minute, and balancing and swinging during the
other two, it is difficult, it is impossible, to keep a
sharp lookout on two persons who are popping at the
other end of the dance. Half of Buckstone Bradford, the worst half, was having a sad time of it,
trying to see over his shoulder and behind his back;
but the other half, the one that had asked Miss
Bethesda to dance, ah! that half was enjoying itself
as it had not done for years. How she danced! as pat

to the music as fiddle to bow! How small her hand looked, just as it used to look, lying in his big brown palm! How — now, where in time were those pesky young ones?

For lo! a thing had happened. At the last triumphant "*pop!*" of the weasel, there had been another pop through the little door at the farther end of the hall; and by this time, Miss Bethesda calculated, Will and Nan must have reached the foot of the back stairs, and be flying across the kitchen on their way to the outer door and safety. She drew a long breath, and turned to her companion, trying to keep the light of triumph out of her eyes. Bradford had stopped short, setting the dancers all astray; he looked around the room, seeking the delinquents; his heavy brows met, his face grew scarlet. Yes, Miss Bethesda knew he would be proper mad! But now he turned, and fixed his eyes on her with relentless scrutiny; another moment, and with a roar like a wild animal, he darted in pursuit.

The fiddler, who had learned more things than fiddling from old De Arthenay, put out his foot, hoping to trip up the angry man; but, heavy as he was, Bradford leaped aside like a deer, and the next instant he was in the outer hall, and Bethesda Pool after him.

"Buckstone," she cried, "wait just a minute, and I'll tell you!"

But he turned on her savagely.

"I'll see to you afterwards, Bethesda Pool!" he cried, furiously. "You won't make me lose time, I can tell you! Think. I don't remember the old short cut? Stand out of the way, or I shall do ye a hurt, and I don't want to do that!"

"Buckstone!" cried Miss Bethesda again; but this time the big man, without another word, lifted her away from the doorway in which she had placed herself, and rushed on.

"He's forgotten," said Miss Bethesda to herself; "he's forgotten, and I didn't tell him. He might—" she caught her breath, for there came the sound of a crash, and then a heavy fall. "Lord, forgive me!" she cried. "He's found it, sure enough, and like t' ha' killed himself."

"It" meant the old trap-door in the room that was formerly used by the Freemasons. Many and many a time had she and Buckstone explored it in childish days, and played prisoner under it, and come up through it in all manner of costume and disguise. He ought to have known the room as well as he knew his own hand. Was it her fault that he had forgotten, in his blind rage? But—but she had seen him rush into the room, and she had not warned him.

"Buckstone, be you hurt?" she cried, leaning over

the dark hole in the floor. She listened, and heard strange sounds from below,—grunts and groans, mingled with unscriptural language.

She drew a long breath. "I knew 'twasn't deep enough to hurt him real bad," she said. "Provided he can cuss, I guess he's all right."

She listened again, inclining her ear this time toward the outer door, and she heard the clear jingle of sleigh-bells and the swish of a sleigh, as it swept out of the yard and away over the snowy road. Again Miss Bethesda breathed deep. "That's a good hearin'," she murmured; "but I *am* sorry for Buckstone!

"Be you hurt?" she asked again, bending once more over the hole.

"I'll let you know whether I'm hurt or not!" muttered Buckstone from below. "Once let me get out of this, and I'll be even with you, Bethesda Pool!"

"Will!" said Miss Bethesda, in her calmest tone. "Well, I must be going, Mr. Bradford. I'll send Iry to help you out. I *am* surprised, though, at you forgettin', after as many times as you've ben down that hole!"

Mr. Bradford's reply did little credit to him as a church-member, and Miss Bethesda, after calling her man and giving him certain directions, returned to her guests in the dancing-hall.

People were looking for her with some curiosity. The news of Will's departure with Nan had spread, and when they saw Buckstone Bradford rush from the room, followed closely by their hostess, there was a good deal of suppressed excitement, but no one dared to follow; you might take liberties with some folks, but Bethesda Pool was not one of them. And, after all, she and Buck Bradford knew each other like two old shoes, if they had n't spoken for fifteen years; and what they — the guests — were here for was a good time, so when the fiddler struck up the "Chorus Jig," most of the dancers took the floor, leaving only a few of the most curious to watch the door, and speculate what was going on behind it. But now the little door opened, and here was Miss Pool again, calm and unruffled, folding her mitted hands, and looking as if she had never heard of such a thing as a runaway couple.

"Why, Bethesdy!" said Mrs. Minchin, taking the freedom of an old schoolmate, "we thought you was lost, for sure, goin' off with Mr. Bradford that way!"

"Did!" replied Miss Bethesda. "Please take your partners to go down to supper!"

The guests, with one exception, were gone. The lights were out in the long ballroom, and the old clock resumed its solitary sway, thankful that the noisy scraping of the fiddle was over. As Miss Bethesda closed the door behind her the clock struck two, and softly, timidly, stole forth the notes of the fairy waltz, as elves, waiting for their forest revels, might steal from their hiding-places when the clumsy foot of man has ceased to echo in their sacred green places. " La-la-la, la-lira-la ! " and who could tell what gentle ghosts were now gliding forward in the dance?

But Miss Bethesda never thought of ghosts. She had to lay a spirit, it was true, but there was little of ghostly about it.

Perhaps she felt some trepidation at the thought of what was before her, and as she listened to Iry's muttered words concerning the mental status of the one guest remaining in the Inn. But she gave no sign, only told Iry to go to bed, and leave his door open, in case she should want to call him.

She took a tray, and covering it with one of her finest napkins, proceeded to lay out a dainty supper, such as she well knew how to prepare. What had Buckstone liked best, in the old times ? She guessed a little of that lobster salad would be about right, and half-a-dozen rolls, feathery and unsubstantial as baked morning cloud ; then a whip, —he always liked a tall whip, with raspberry jam at the bottom ! and a slice of plum-cake, and, — well, a glass of cherry-brandy might do no harm, if they *were* both temperance folks.

He'd be some tired, likely, raging and routing round the way he had been, from what Iry said. And so Miss Bethesda, like the bold woman she was, unlocked the sitting-room door, and entered the lion's den.

She expected a rush, and held her tray firmly; but no rush came. The lion was sitting huddled up in a great chair, with his foot on another chair before him. At first Miss Bethesda thought he was asleep; but catching the sombre glare of his dark eyes, she set the tray down carefully, and faced her guest with folded hands and apparent composure.

"How are you feeling, Mr. Bradford?" she asked, seeing, with some compunction, how pale he was.

"My leg is broke!" was the grim reply, "and I'm injured some inside, most probably bleeding; but otherwise I'm well, Miss Pool, and much obleeged to *you!*"

"You're welcome!" said Bethesda, with a flash; and then she went down on her knees, and manipulated him skilfully.

"Your leg is n't broke!" she announced, cheerfully; "but you have got a leetle sprain into your ankle, Buck, — I should say Mr. Bradford, — and it's some considerable swoll up. You'd better let me bathe it for ye, and then have a bit of supper, and then you can lay right down on the l'unge here, and rest ye till morning. You'll be all right by then, I calc'late, and able to git you home, — with a stick!"

The last thrust was pure malice, and the big man winced; but not altogether at thought of the stick or the sprained ankle.

"I've got no home," he said; "thanks to you, Bethesda Pool! You've seen that my girl got off safe with that good-for-nothin' feller, and that's the last of any home for me! I hope it's done ye good!"

"It has so!" replied Miss Bethesda, rubbing the ankle briskly with her favourite liniment. "A sight o' good it's done me, Mr. Bradford, and I hope 't will do you good, too, some day!"

"May I ask," Buckstone continued, grimly, glowering down on the little woman, as she knelt beside him, "why you felt called to make or meddle in my affairs, Miss Bethesda Pool?"

"You may!" said Miss Bethesda, looking up with fire in her eye. "Your girl, pretty creetur, come cryin' to me the other day, and told me all about how you was treating her, Buckstone Bradford; and 't was a shame, and you know it was! There's nothing in this world against Will Newell, well you know! He's a church-member, and he's well thought of by all that's acquainted with him. You did n't like his father, because you thought I,— because you thought things about him that there was no occasion for thinking, and he killed in the war afterwards and all; and that's all the reason, save

and except that you are a greedy grab-all, Buckstone
Bradford, and don't want your girl to do anything all
her days 'cept wait on you! That's the living truth,
and you know it as well as I do! Hurt ye, did I?
Well, I'm sorry for that, but if I could hurt your mind
instead of your ankle, I should be pleased to death!
I can speak when I've a mind to, if they do call me a
dummy; and I'm speaking to you now, Buckstone,
and don't you forget it! You've been acting mean
and selfish and greedy, and every right-thinking
person in this village is disgusted with you, clean
through to the ground! So, now! And I helped
them children off for pure pleasure, so I did, and for
love of seeing young things happy, if I aint ben
happy myself! Not that that's here or there. I
planned this party for it, and laid out consid'able
money, and set every tongue in the village clacking
till they c'enamost dropped off, and a mighty good
thing, too, if they had! and I sent for Will Newell,
and showed him where he could hitch his hoss, and
how he could git his girl off the quickest and the
safest. You was pretty spry, Buckstone, but you
would n't ha' caught 'em, even if you had n't — if you
had n't have fell down the Tumplety Hole. And —
and that's what I did, and glad clean through to my
back-comb that I done it, and would do it again the
fust time I got a chance!"

Miss Bethesda paused for breath, and bound up the lame ankle, wrapping it in fold on fold of cool linen. She expected thunders of reply, but Buckstone Bradford was silent.

There was a long pause, during which the coals tinkled in the grate and the frost cracked and snapped outside.

At length,—"The Tumplety Hole!" he said, musingly. "Yès, that was it! I was trying to think what we used to call it, and I could n't bring the name to mind. The Tumplety Hole, sure enough! And you come up through it, one day, dressed in a white gown with silver trimmin's,—"

"That I found in the old trunk up garret!" put in Miss Bethesda.

"And flowers in your hair!" Bradford went on. "I thought you looked the slickest of anything I ever saw, then, Bethesda; and — well, I don't know but I think so still."

"Foolishness!" said Miss Bethesda, rising and wiping her hands. "Have a bit o' supper, now, Buckstone, do!"

"No, I could n't eat," said the big man, drawing his hand slowly across his brow. "I could n't eat your victuals, Bethesda, and have you thinkin' of me the way you—you said. It's all true, it seems born in on me to feel. I've done a good bit o' thinkin', sittin' here alone. I never realized it before, but the fact seems to be that I've been a hog, and bein' so, I can't sit down with no lady and eat her victuals, you see."

"Foolishness!" said Miss Bethesda again, looking rather discomposed. "You mustn't think too much of what I said, Buckstone. Mebbe I spoke too hash—"

"Oh, you spoke out!" said the man. "Need n't ever anybody tell me that Bethesda Pool can't open her head. When them waters is troubled, there's no mistake about their movin'; I knowed that before. You spoke out once before to me, Bethesda, and the sound of it stays with me yet. There! I guess I'll be goin'. You said you'd lend me a stick, did ye?"

"Good Isick!" cried Miss Bethesda, standing up to bar his way, in real distress. "Buckstone, you can't go out in this cold in the middle of the night, and with your ankle that way. You'll ketch your death. Stop where you be, like a sensible man, and have some supper with me!"

"S'pose I do ketch my death!" said Buckstone; "aint no one to care, that I know of. Nan's gone, and there's no one else, is there, Bethesda?"

"Good Isick!" cried Miss Bethesda again, and wrung her hands in sheer desperation. Whither were they drifting?

"If I thought—" Buckstone Bradford was speaking again, slowly this time, the anger clean gone out of him, but with an earnestness that shook his deep voice, and made the brave little woman before him tremble, and her cheek flush as it had not done for many a day—

"If I thought there *was* anyone that cared what become of me; if I thought there was anyone that was willing to let bygones be bygones, seeing that I've cared for that person all my life, since —since first we knew there was a Tumplety Hole in that room; if I thought there was anyone who knew she could fetch out all the good there was in me,—in old "Gruff and Grum,"—and that knew best of anyone how much good there was to be fetched—why—if there *was* any such person, I'd sit down to that table the proudest man in the wide world, and the happiest! But—but—I don't suppose there is, do you, Bethesda?"

"Oh, my gracious land of deliverance!" cried Miss Bethesda, fairly beside herself. "I—I—don't know as there is, Buckstone, and—and yet—I don't know *but* there is! But do, for gracious sake, sit down, whatever way it is, and eat your supper like a Christian man!"

And Buckstone sat down.

THE END.